Clever Little
Freddy

For Frank and Amanda
- C.L.

For Mum and Dad
- J.M.

This edition produced 2003 for
The Travelling Book Company
Troubadour Limited, Express House, Crow Arch Lane
Ringwood, Hampshire BH24 1PD, by
LITTLE TIGER PRESS
An imprint of Magi Publications,
1 The Coda Centre, 189 Munster Road, London SW6 6AW
www.littletigerpress.com
First published in Great Britain 1997

Clever Little Freddy

by Christine Leeson

illustrated by Joanne Moss

THE TRAVELLING BOOK COMPANY

One crisp, star-frosted night Mrs Fox gathered her three cubs together outside the den.
"I think it's time you all learned to hunt," she told them. "Tonight you can try to catch your own suppers."

Frannie and Rennie were very excited. They frisked and jumped and tore off into the woods to stalk mice. But they were clumsy and noisy and they didn't catch a single one. Rennie even got bitten on the nose!

"I'm not catching any silly mice," said Freddy. "I'm much too clever to bother with all that chasing. I'll let my supper come to me."

Freddy trotted briskly through the woods until he reached the road. His mother had often told him to stay away, but Freddy knew there were sometimes tasty treats by the side of it. A car sped past. Something pale and fluttering flew out of its window and landed at Freddy's feet. Was it alive?

It didn't move but smelt delicious. It even *tasted* delicious.

"There, what did I say!" cried Freddy. "A lovely supper and no work. What a clever little fox I am!" And feeling very pleased with himself, he trotted home.

"Well, how did you get on?" asked Mrs Fox, when the cubs returned to the den.
Freddy stepped proudly forward with his catch.
"That's *human's* food!" cried Mrs Fox. She glared at Freddy but she couldn't be cross for long.
There wasn't much meat on the worm and the beetle that Frannie and Rennie had caught. It was very clever of Freddy to find the tastiest supper of all.

Freddy wandered on down to the river bank.
A fisherman sat there, with a tempting picnic
basket by his side.

"Delicious!" thought the young fox, licking his
lips. He waited until the fisherman had dozed
off and then he crept up to the basket and
grabbed the food. Just in time!

As Freddy sneaked away, the fisherman
yawned and opened his eyes.

"You tried your best," Mrs Fox told Frannie and
  Rennie when the cubs returned to the den.
  They had brought her a snail and a tail feather.
"Look what I've got!" said Freddy.
"That isn't prey!" cried Mrs Fox. "You didn't hunt it."
"I sneaked up on it ever so quietly," said Freddy.
"It nearly got away."
"You're too clever for your own good," said Mrs Fox.
          "You'll be in big trouble one day,
              you mark my words!"

The next evening Mrs Fox sent the cubs out to catch rabbits. Off went Frannie and Rennie into the fields, where the rabbits' white bobtails shone like stars in the dusk.

Frannie followed one of them down a rabbit hole and got stuck. Rennie had to pull her out by the tail.

"Stupid things!" thought Freddy. "I'm not going to waste my time catching rabbits. *I* know where there's even juicier food."

Off Freddy trotted towards the farmyard.
He peered through the fence and could see a nice,
plump gosling, sitting in a pool of bright moonlight.
"Yummy!" said Freddy. "Just waiting for me."
Very quietly, he crawled towards the gosling . . .

one step . . .

two steps . . .

three steps . . .

At that moment, everything happened at once.
The gosling squealed. The farmyard dog barked,
and all the other geese came running towards him,
hissing and honking and snapping.
Freddy looked for a way of escape. He saw a gap
and ran out through the gate, as fast as his four
paws could carry him.

Freddy ran and ran until he reached the woods.
The geese and the dog were close behind him
and Freddy thought his last moment had come.
But then something happened.

A streak of red fur
launched itself on
the pursuing animals,
barking and snarling.
There was a flurry of
fur and feathers and
before Freddy knew
what was happening,
Mrs Fox ran out from the fighting mass.
"Run, you silly little fox, run!" she cried.

Freddy and his mother both ran and ran
until the noise of the geese and the
dog was far behind them.

A little later, Freddy and his mother arrived
back at the den.

"What have you caught?" asked Frannie.

"Freddy nearly got caught himself," said Mrs Fox,
as she told them what had happened.

"Stupid Freddy!" laughed Rennie and Frannie.
"Serves you right for being too clever."

"You're not as clever as you think you are,"
scolded Mrs Fox. "Off you go to bed now, before
you get into any more trouble!"

Freddy crept quietly into the corner
of the den to sleep and was soon
hunting again – but only
in his dreams.

More books for you to enjoy from

The Travelling Books Reading Library

The Healthy Wolf
David Bedford
& Mandy Stanley

Charlie & Tess
Martin Hall
& Catherine Walters

The Great Goat Chase
Tony Bonning
& Sally Hobson

George and Sylvia
Michael Coleman
& Tim Warnes

It Could Have Been Worse
AH Benjamin
& Tim Warnes

The Long Journey Home
David Bedford
& Penny Ives

Don't be Afraid, Little One
Caroline Pitcher
& Jane Chapman

Titus's Troublesome Tooth
Linda Jennings
& Gwyneth Williamson

Davy's Scary Journey
Christine Leeson
& Tim Warnes

Run Little Fawn, Run!
Sheridan Cain
& Gavin Rowe

One, Two, Three, Oops!
Michael Coleman
& Gwyneth Williamson

Sleepy Sam
Michael Catchpool
& Eleanor Taylor

Lazy Ozzie
Michael Coleman
& Gwyneth Williamson

Ridiculous!
Michael Coleman
& Gwyneth Williamson

TRAVELLING BOOKS
READING LIBRARY